David Walliams

PRESENTS...

For Heath
and his gorgeous smile,
with love,
David x

For Robbie,
with love,
Adam x

First published in hardback by HarperCollins *Children's Books* in 2022
HarperCollins *Children's Books* is a division of HarperCollins *Publishers* Ltd
1 London Bridge Street, London SE1 9GF
HarperCollins*Publishers*,
1st Floor, Watermarque Building, Ringsend Road, Dublin 4, Ireland
Text copyright © David Walliams 2022. Illustrations copyright © Adam Stower 2022
Cover lettering of author's name copyright © Quentin Blake 2010
1 3 5 7 9 10 8 6 4 2
David Walliams and Adam Stower assert the moral right to be identified
as the author and illustrator of the work.
A CIP catalogue record for this title is available from the British Library.
Printed and bound in Italy
978-0-00-830575-8

This book belongs to:

MARMALADE
THE ORANGE PANDA

ILLUSTRATED
BY THE AMAZING
Adam
Stower

HarperCollins *Children's Books*

One morning, deep in the forest, a beautiful
baby panda was born.

This panda was different to all the others,
as he had dazzling <u>orange</u> fur.

The baby's mummy was surprised.
Pandas are always white with black bits
or black with white bits.

However, she couldn't be more in LOVE.

"I will call you . . . Marmalade!" she whispered as she cradled her first-born in her arms.

Soon ALL the pandas in the forest woke up. They gathered around to see the newest member of their embarrassment. YES! A group of pandas really IS called that! An *embarrassment* of pandas!

"No! NO! NOO!" said the Elder Panda. "This odd-looking bear does NOT belong with us!"

"But **why?**" protested his mum.

"He is an **embarrassment** to the EMBARRASSMENT!"

"HEAR! HEAR!" agreed the others.

"Marmalade is **absolutely perfect!**" she said.
A **tear** rolled down her cheek.
It **landed** on her son's **nose**. *PLIP!*

Marmalade **looked up** to see his mum
crying and felt **sad** himself.

Perhaps the other pandas are right,
he thought. *Perhaps I don't fit in here.*

While his mum gathered bamboo shoots, Marmalade stole himself off **alone** to the **river**. He gazed down at his **reflection**. The other pandas *were* **right**. He *was* **different**.

So he decided to take himself off to see where he might **belong**. Marmalade **hopped** on to a **log** . . . DOINK!

. . . and began **bobbing** along the river.

The log *slid* down a waterfall.

SPLOSH!

Then, as the river widened and slowed, the baby panda spotted all the weird and wonderful creatures of the forest for the very first time.

Wolves slurping.

Leopards *lurking*.

Alligators splashing and sploshing.

Suddenly Marmalade found himself being *WHISKED* up in the air.

WHOOSH!

A pair of **monkeys** was **hiding** in a tree.

"Is it a monkey?"   "NO!"

"But it **looks** like **us!**"

"It's **orange!** That's all! Drop it **back** in the **river!**"

WHOOSH!

Just before Marmalade **hit the water**, he was **caught** in the beak of an **ibis**.

SNAP!

The bird **soared** high above the tops of the trees to join its **congregation** in flight.

FLAP!

FLAP!

FLAP!

"Is it **one** of us?"

"Funny-looking **bird** if it is!"

"Look at its **colour**. It's like **us**!"

"**Nothing** like us!"

"Put it **back** where you **found** it!"

With that, the ibis **dropped** the baby panda from its beak.

WHIZZ!

Marmalade fell through the trees and **landed** on the **back** of a sleeping tiger!

THUMP!

"ROAR!"

The startled **tiger** *darted* through the forest.
Marmalade held on **tight** to the **tiger's ears**, *thrilled* by the **ride**.

BUMPETY!

The tiger **stopped** at a clearing where a **streak** of the huge **orange cats** was waiting.

"**LOOK!** A tiger cub!"

"Don't be daft! That's **NOT** a tiger!"

"What *is* it, then?"

"I think it's a panda!"

"Pandas aren't orange!"

"Let's **EAT** it and find out!"

The tigers began licking their lips.

SLURP!

SLURP!

SLURP!

NOT wanting to be a tigers' all-you-can-eat buffet,
Marmalade **raced up** the nearest tree.

SCUTTLE!

He made his **escape**, hopping from **branch** to branch
as the **hungry tigers ROARED** from the ground.

"ROAR!"   "ROAR!"   "ROAR!"

When he was sure he had lost them,
Marmalade *slid* down,
BANGING his bottom
on every branch.

BOINK!

BOINK!

BOINK!

Next, he traced his way home
along the riverbank.

Marmalade leaped over
the jaws of a peckish
pangolin . . .

SNAP!

... and *slid* down a sinister snake ...

"HISS!"

... before bouncing off the belly of a moody moon bear!

"GROWL!"

BOING!

Marmalade *flew* through the **air** . . .

. . . landing in a HUGE muddy puddle.

Marmalade **looked down** at his **fur**.

Now he had **dark patches** like **all** the **other pandas.**

Delighted that he would now **fit in**,
Marmalade **bounded** all the way **home.**

It was **night** by the time Marmalade reached the **embarrassment**.
All the pandas were **sleeping**, except **one**.
His mum.

The poor panda looked **worried** sick.

When Marmalade approached, she **didn't**
recognise him at **first**, but then . . .

"Marmalade? Can that be **you**?" she asked as she *rushed* towards her baby and **scooped** him up in her **arms**. "Oh! Marmalade! I looked **everywhere** in the forest for **you**! I thought you had run away **forever**!

But **tell me**, what has **happened** to your **wonderful orange fur**?"

She patted him with her paw and **clouds** of **dusty mud** **exploded** into the **air**.

WHOOF!

"Oh, my darling Marmalade!" said Mum. "You **never** need to **change**! You are **perfect** just as you are!"

To help the baby panda understand, she picked some brightly coloured forest flowers and rubbed her paws along them. "Look! I could be blue or pink or purple and I would STILL be your mum!"

Little Marmalade bounced up and down in excitement.

BOING! BOING! BOING!

He put his hand on a bright yellow flower and rubbed the dust of colour on to his mother's fur. They giggled together.

"HA! HA! HA!"

They both looked over to the sleeping pandas.

"ZZZZ!   ZZZZ!   ZZZZ!"

"Are you thinking what I'm thinking?"
she whispered.

Marmalade eagerly
nodded his head.

WIBBLE!

WOBBLE!

"*Shush!* Let's be quiet, though. We don't want
to wake them all up. Well, not yet!"

Marmalade and Mum gathered as many different brightly
coloured plants and flowers from the forest as they could.

Soon they had great handfuls of powdery paint.

As all the other pandas slept, the pair went to work.
One sleeping panda they painted purple.

Another they painted pink.

But they saved the BEST until last . . .

One they painted blue.

Another they painted green.

Mum painted herself red.

While the Elder Panda snored away, the pair giggled as they painted him every colour of the RAINBOW!

"ZZZZ! ZZZZ! ZZZZ!"

"TEE! HEE! HEE!"

So, when dawn rose over the forest, ALL the pandas awoke
to find themselves painted the craziest colours.

"WHAT is the MEANING of this?"
thundered the Elder Panda.

But he looked SO funny that ALL the other pandas laughed.

"HA! HA! HA!"

Looking down at his multicoloured tummy, the Elder Panda couldn't help but burst out laughing too. "HA! HA! You were RIGHT! It doesn't matter if we are different –

we ALL belong TOGETHER!"

"HOORAY!" cheered the whole embarrassment, not the least bit *embarrassed* any more.

Mum and Marmalade shared a smile before leading the multicoloured pandas in a celebratory parade around the forest.

"HOOO!"

Soon ALL the other animals joined in the party.

A moon bear painted herself maroon.
A leopard dusted his fur lime green.
A snake made herself canary yellow.

Thanks to a little orange panda, every animal in the forest
was happy being themselves.

But no one
was happier than
Marmalade.